WORLD IN
FOCUS

FOCUS ON
SWEDEN

NICOLA BARBER

WORLD ALMANAC® LIBRARY

Please visit our web site at: www.garethstevens.com
For a free color catalog describing World Almanac® Library's list of high-quality books
and multimedia programs, call 1-800-848-2928 (USA) or 1-800-387-3178 (Canada).
World Almanac® Library's fax: (414) 332-3567.

Library of Congress Cataloging-in-Publication Data

Barber, Nicola.
    Focus on Sweden / Nicola Barber. — North American ed.
        p. cm. — (World in focus)
    Includes bibliographical references and index.
    ISBN-13: 978-0-8368-6739-8 (lib. bdg.)
    ISBN-13: 978-0-8368-6746-6 (softcover)
    1. Sweden—Juvenile literature. I. Title.
    DL609.B27   2007
    948.5—dc22   2006027633

This North American edition first published in 2007 by
World Almanac® Library
A Member of the WRC Media Family of Companies
330 West Olive Street, Suite 100
Milwaukee, WI 53212 USA

This U.S. edition copyright © 2007 by World Almanac® Library. Original edition
copyright © 2006 by Hodder Wayland. First published in 2006 by Wayland, an imprint
of Hachette Children's Books, 338 Euston Road, London NW1 3BH, U.K.

Commissioning editor: Nicola Edwards
Editor: Patience Coster
Inside design: Chris Halls, www.mindseyedesign.co.uk
Cover design: Hodder Wayland
Series concept and project management by EASI-Educational Resourcing
(info@easi-er.co.uk)
Statistical research: Anna Bowden
Maps and graphs: Martin Darlison, Encompass Graphics

World Almanac® Library editor: Alan Wachtel
World Almanac® Library cover design: Scott Krall

Picture acknowledgements. The author and publisher would like to thank the following for allowing their pictures to be reproduced
in this publication:
Alamy 20 (Nordicphotos), 27 (Pixonnet.com), 29 (Bjorn Svensson), 40 (Frank Chmura), 42 (Chad Ehlers), 44 (Stock Connection
Distribution), 56 (Martin Bond); Corbis 4 (Hans Strand), 6 (Wolfgang Rattay/Reuters), 9 (Macduff Everton), 10 (Macduff Everton),
cover (top) and 11 (Macduff Everton), 12 (The Art Archive), 13 (Peter Turnley), 14 (Hubert Stadler), 16 (Jorma Jaemsen/Zefa),
17 (Anders Ryman), 19 (Bo Zaunders), 21 (Fridmar Damm/Zefa), 25 (Steve Raymer), 28 (Alexander Benz/Zefa), 31 (Frederic Pitchal),
33 (Steve Raymer), 35 (Hulton-Deutsch Collection), 37 (Stefan Lindblom), 43 (Anders Ryman), 45 (Zwalm dan Vander),
46 (Historical Picture Archive), 47 (Denis O'Regan), 49 (Anders Ryman), title page and 50 (Hans Strand), 51 (Tony Gentile/Reuters),
52 (US Air Force), cover (bottom) and 53 (Hans Strand), 54 (Staffan Widstrand), 59 (Blaine Harrington III); Corbis Sygma 24 (Lena
Ulvenstam); EASI-Images (Rob Bowden) 38; EASI-Images (Edward Parker) 5, 8, 15, 18, 22, 23, 26, 30, 32, 34, 36, 39, 41, 48, 55, 57, 58.

The directional arrow portrayed on the map on page 7 provides only an approximation of north.
The data used to produce the graphics and data panels in this title were the latest available at the time of production.

Printed in China

1 2 3 4 5 6 7 8 9 10 09 08 07 06

CONTENTS

Cover: Kalmar Slott (Kalmar Castle) stands on a small island off Sweden's east coast.

Title page: A hiker sits on a rock above the Rapa River Valley in Sarek National Park.

CHAPTER 1

Sweden – An Overview

Sweden is part of Scandinavia, the group of northern European countries that also includes Norway and Denmark. It is the largest Scandinavian country, and it is very prosperous, with a high standard of living. The Swedes are extremely proud of their country, with its vast areas of unspoiled landscape, its beautiful coastline, its rich natural resources, and its long history.

Sweden is a long, narrow country that extends north beyond the Arctic Circle. This means that in its northernmost regions there is 24-hour darkness for a period during the winter and 24-hour sunlight at midsummer. Its landscapes include the dramatic mountain ranges of the northwest, extensive forests and lakes, the rocky coastline of the west, and the wide plains of the south. The Swedes love outdoor activities and make great use of the natural attractions of their country. Fishing, skiing, and cycling are among some of the most popular outdoor pursuits among Swedes.

▼ Children play under a sea stack in Fårö, Sweden, a small island to the north of Gotland in the Baltic Sea. Sea stacks such as these have been carved out of soft limestone rock by wind and waves.

SWEDEN AND ITS NEIGHBORS

Sweden has close ties with its nearest neighbors—Norway, Finland, and Denmark. It shares land borders with both Norway and Finland, and the narrow sea strait between Denmark and Sweden has recently been bridged by the Öresund Link. The histories of Sweden and its neighbors are closely intertwined. Sweden, Norway and Denmark were united under one monarch in 1397, and Finland was part of Sweden until 1809. Norway was united once again with Sweden during the nineteenth century, until its independence in 1905.

SWEDEN'S CITIES

The vast majority of Sweden's population lives in the southern part of the country, and the country's biggest cities are located in this region. Sweden's capital is the beautiful city of Stockholm, which is situated in an archipelago on the Baltic coast. The second biggest city in Sweden is Göteborg, located on its west coast. Nicknamed by its residents the "face of Sweden," Göteborg has long acted as a gateway to Sweden for the outside world. It is a major industrial city and home to the Swedish car manufacturer Volvo. The country's third biggest city, Malmö, is on the south coast. Like both Stockholm and Göteborg, Malmö is a major port with many high-tech industries, including, for example, companies specializing in information technology. The opening of the Öresund Link between Malmö and Copenhagen, Denmark, in 2000 was a major landmark in the city's history.

 Did You Know?

The Swedish national anthem celebrates the beauty of the country, hailing Sweden as the "loveliest land on the Earth."

▼ This aerial view of Sweden's capital, Stockholm, is taken from the Kaknäs Television Tower.

A DEMOCRATIC NATION

Sweden is a parliamentary democracy with a monarch as its head of state. Since 1917, the monarch has had no real political power (although this was not formalized until 1974). He or she is, however, considered to be important as a representative for Sweden, and the royal family is very popular. Democracy and equality are extremely important principles in Sweden. Great emphasis has been placed on equality between men and women in Swedish society. There is a high proportion of women in Sweden's parliament, and the welfare system provides generous support to allow both men and women to work after the birth of a child. Sweden's welfare system, which covers areas such as health care, education, child care, pensions, and care of the elderly, is one of the most extensive in the world. It is paid for by high taxes. Most Swedes are proud of the way their country takes care of all of its people according to their needs.

Physical Geography

- 🗀 Land area: 158,620 sq miles/410,934 sq km
- 🗀 Water area: 15,066 sq miles/39,030 sq km
- 🗀 Total area: 173,686 sq miles/449,964 sq km
- 🗀 World rank (by area): 55
- 🗀 Land boundaries: 1,388 miles/2,233 km
- 🗀 Border countries: Finland, Norway
- 🗀 Coastline: 2,000 miles/3,218 km
- 🗀 Highest point: Kebnekaise (6,926 ft/2,111 m)
- 🗀 Lowest point: reclaimed bay of Lake Hammarsjon, near Kristianstad (-7.9 ft/-2.41 m)

Source: CIA World Factbook

Focus on: Sweden's National Day

Since 2005, Sweden's national day, June 6, has been declared a public holiday. This date was chosen as a national day for two reasons: it was the day in 1523 when Gustav Vasa was elected king of Sweden, and it was the day in 1809 on which Sweden adopted a new constitution. The country's national day has been celebrated every year since 1916.

 Did You Know?

The design of Sweden's flag dates from the sixteenth century. Its design is probably taken from the Danish flag.

◀ Members of Sweden's royal family arrive for the Nobel Dinner in Stockholm in 2004. On the left is Crown Princess Victoria, heir to the throne, and on the right is her younger brother, Prince Carl Philip. They are escorting their great aunt, Princess Lilian.

CHAPTER 2

History

Fourteen thousand years ago, the whole of the country we now know as Sweden was covered by thick ice. Gradually, the ice began to melt, and, as it retreated northward, humans followed onto the newly revealed land. The earliest known human habitation in Sweden, in the south of the country, dates from about 12,000 B.C. The first settlers were hunters and fishers who made stone tools. After about 1800 B.C., bronze weapons and other objects became widespread, and after about 500 B.C. ironworking began in the region. Settled communities became established as people started to farm the land.

THE SUIONES

The early Swedes were intrepid sailors, and as early as 1500 B.C, they had extensive trade routes as far south as the Danube River.

Archaeological finds in Sweden show that trade with the Roman Empire, far to the south, later became well established. In A.D. 98 the Roman historian Tacitus described the Swedes as a tribe of people called the Suiones, who lived on an "island" in the Baltic and had powerful fleets of ships with prows at both ends, "so that the boat can advance head-on in either direction."

THE SWEDISH VIKINGS

From about A.D. 800, people from southern Scandinavia (present-day Sweden, Denmark, and Norway) started to raid and conquer lands overseas. These people spoke a language called Norse, and they became known as Vikings,

▼ These Bronze Age rock carvings at Tanumshede, located on the west coast of Sweden, show ships and battles, as well as hunting and fishing scenes.

from the Norse word *vik* for "bay" or "inlet." It is thought that the Viking expansion was partly a result of overpopulation at home. The Swedish Vikings headed east across the Baltic Sea and along rivers that took them deep into Russia, where they traded for warm furs and amber. They crossed the Black Sea to reach Constantinople (now Istanbul), the capital of the Byzantine Empire, from where they brought back gold, silver, and luxury cloths.

 Did You Know?

The Latin word *Suiones* is similar to the Anglo-Saxon *Sweon*, from which the English word *Sweden* is derived. The Swedes' own name for their country is Sverige, meaning "Land of the Svears." This name refers to the group of people who first settled in the region around Lake Mälaren and gradually came to dominate most of the country.

Focus on: A Viking Town

The town of Birka lies on the island of Björkö, located west of present-day Stockholm. It was founded in the late eighth century and abandoned about 200 years later, although it is not clear why. Excavations of this Viking town have revealed that it was well protected, with defensive ramparts and a fortress to house its people if the town was attacked. It is thought that between 500 and 1,000 people lived in Birka, and about 1,600 burial sites have been discovered in its area. According to Norse beliefs, people were buried with objects that could be useful in the life after death. In these graves, archaeologists have found weapons; food and drink; clothes, including fine furs and Oriental silks; Arabic coins; pottery; and glass. All of these finds point to the immense wealth of this trading town.

► These grave markers on Öland Island, located off the east coast of Sweden, date from the Iron Age. The windmill in the distance is one of about 400 windmills that stand on the island.

THE ARRIVAL OF CHRISTIANITY

Christianity arrived in Sweden in 829 with the missionary Ansgar, who came from Germany. It was not until the eleventh century, however, that the Christian faith began to gain popularity over the traditional beliefs of the Norse religion. At about the same time, Denmark, Norway, and Sweden began to emerge as separate kingdoms. By 1249, most of Finland was under the control of Sweden, after campaigns led by successive Swedish kings.

THE HANSEATIC LEAGUE

In the thirteenth and fourteenth centuries, the Hanseatic League (Hansa) rose in importance in Sweden. This was a powerful alliance of German trading cities under the leadership of the city of Lübeck. Hanseatic traders established an important base at Visby, on Gotland. Other trading towns, including Stockholm, also developed during this period.

The German merchants dominated trade in the Baltic area. German influence was felt throughout the region in architecture, fashions, and even in the Swedish language, which absorbed many German words.

THE KALMAR UNION

In 1350, disaster struck Sweden in the form of the bubonic plague, also known as the Black Death, which killed one-third of the population of the country. Many farms were abandoned because there were not enough people to work the land. This crisis, coupled with concerns about the power of the Hansa, led to the Kalmar Union in 1397, in which Sweden, Norway, and Denmark were united under

▼ Women wear traditional clothes during a medieval reenactment in Visby. Visby is located on Gotland Island, off Sweden's east coast.

the same monarch. The Kalmar Union lasted for over a century, but it was marked by conflict in Sweden between those who supported it and those who opposed it. In 1520, 80 leading Swedish noblemen were executed in Stockholm —the so-called "Stockholm Bloodbath"—on the orders of the Danish union king, Kristian II. This act prompted a revolt, led by the Swedish nobleman Gustav Eriksson Vasa, that brought the Kalmar Union to an end in 1521. Two years later, Gustav was crowned king of Sweden.

THE VASAS

Gustav I Vasa (reigned 1523–1560) proved to be a powerful and effective monarch, laying the foundations of the modern country of Sweden. He confiscated the property and land of the Roman Catholic Church and supported the introduction of the Reformation into Sweden, making Lutheranism the official religion. He also strengthened the power of the monarchy.

Swedish kings had always been elected, but this process led to power struggles between the nobles. In 1544, Gustav made the monarchy hereditary, meaning that on his death the Crown would automatically pass to his eldest son. This resulted in the Vasa dynasty continuing for more than one hundred years, in spite of challenges from the nobles.

 Did You Know?

The first Swedish king to accept the Christian faith was King Olof Skötkonung, who was baptized in 1008.

▼ Kalmar Slott (Kalmar Castle), protected by walls and bastions, stands on a small island along the Slottsfjarden on Sweden's east coast. The Kalmar Union was proclaimed in this castle.

EMPIRE BUILDING

Under the rule of the Vasas, Sweden expanded its territories through a series of wars. Gustav II Adolf (reigned 1611–1632) was a particularly brilliant military leader who won battles against Denmark, Poland, and Russia. He involved Sweden in the Thirty Years War (1618–1648), a religious conflict between Catholics and Protestants that affected most of Europe. Gustav II Adolf was killed on the battlefield at Lützen, Germany. By the middle of the seventeenth century, Sweden was a powerful force in northern Europe, controlling a large empire that extended across much of Scandinavia and into Russia. It even briefly had a small colony in North America on the Delaware River. But Sweden's economy was still based on agriculture, and it lacked the resources to maintain its position. During the Napoleonic Wars at the beginning of the nineteenth century, Sweden lost much of its empire. It did, however, gain Norway, which was united with Sweden from 1814 until 1905.

MASS EMIGRATION

Sweden adopted a policy of neutrality in 1812. In spite of this, the country fought a short war with Norway in 1814—the last time it became directly involved in a war. Peace and stability during the nineteenth century led to a massive increase in Sweden's population—from 1.8 million in 1750 to 3.5 million in 1850. However, lack of jobs, failed harvests, and famine forced many Swedes to leave their country. Between 1851 and 1930, nearly 1.5 million Swedes emigrated. Most went to start new lives in North America. The resulting fall in the country's population led directly to the establishment of national policies to help women combine work and family life—and, thus, to promote population growth.

Focus on: Queen Kristina

When Gustav II Adolf died in 1632, his six-year-old daughter, Kristina, succeeded him to the throne. Until she came of age, her father's chancellor, Axel Oxenstierna, ruled Sweden and continued Gustav's exploits abroad. When she was old enough, Queen Kristina ruled over a glittering court that attracted artists and scholars from all over Europe. Despite her Protestant upbringing, Kristina was attracted to the Roman Catholic faith. In 1654, she abdicated and left Sweden for Rome, where she converted to Catholicism. Kristina was the last monarch of the Vasa dynasty.

◀ Gustav II Adolf was one of Sweden's greatest kings. He is sometimes referred to as "the Lion of the North."

INDUSTRIALIZATION

In the late nineteenth and early twentieth centuries, Sweden's economy industrialized rapidly. Trade unions were established, and the right to vote was given to men in 1909 and to women in 1921. During the two world wars that tore Europe apart during the twentieth century, Sweden held fast to its policy of neutrality. The welfare state, which was set up after World War II, helped to provide financial security and essential services for all Swedes, with provisions such as unemployment payments and free childcare. During the 1950s and 1960s, living standards in Sweden improved dramatically, fueled by the country's booming economy.

▼ Mourners gather in the streets of Stockholm for the funeral of Olof Palme in 1986.

AN OPEN SOCIETY

In 1986, people in Sweden and across the world were stunned to learn of the assassination of Sweden's prime minister, Olof Palme, on the streets of Stockholm. No one knows who committed the murder, but, in the aftermath, many Swedes stressed the continuing importance of the egalitarian and nonviolent values that lie at the heart of their society and culture. These values were once again emphasized in 2003, following the equally shocking murder, also in Stockholm, of Foreign Minister Anna Lindh. In both cases, one of the reasons the killers had been able to target their victims was because Sweden lacked heavy security for its leading politicians. Protection for prominent public figures in Sweden has been tightened since Anna Lindh's murder.

CHAPTER 3

Landscape and Climate

Sweden covers a total area of 173,686 square miles (449,964 square kilometers). It is a long, thin country, with a maximum distance of 978 miles (1,574 km) from north to south and 310 miles (499 km) from east to west. It has a long, rugged coastline that stretches from the Gulf of Bothnia in the north to the Baltic Sea in the south and to the Kattegat (the channel that lies between Sweden and Denmark) in the west. There are many islands off Sweden's coast. The two largest are Gotland and Öland, which lie in the Baltic Sea. Sweden's mainland has a variety of landscapes, from the rugged mountains of the northwest to the fertile plains of the southeast. The country has thousands of lakes, the largest of which are Vänern (2,155 sq miles/5,584 sq km) and Vättern (738 sq miles/1,911 sq km).

NORRLAND

Sweden's terrain is divided into three main regions: Norrland, Svealand, and Götaland. Norrland covers the northern three-fifths of the

▼ A river valley in Sarek National Park in Norrland. This park is an area of mountain wilderness that covers 486,787 acres (197,000 hectares).

country. In the west of this region, the Kölen Mountains form the border between Sweden and Norway. Sweden's highest point, Kebnekaise (Mount Kebne) is among these mountains and reaches 6,926 feet (2,111 meters). Sweden's largest rivers originate in the Kölen Mountains and flow southeast across the Northern Highlands to the Gulf of Bothnia. The Northern Highlands is a sparsely populated area of forest, rivers, and lakes, with fertile valleys opening out towards the coast.

The far north of Norrland lies well within the Arctic Circle, so people in this region experience long summer days and long winter nights. In fact, during the month of June there is 24-hour daylight because the sun never dips below the horizon. But in midwinter—from mid-December to mid-January—there is 24-hour darkness because the sun does not appear above the horizon. During these days of darkness, the aurora borealis, or the northern lights, can often be seen illuminating the sky with spectacular and colorful displays.

SVEALAND AND GÖTALAND

South of Norrland lies Svealand, or the "Land of the Svears." This region is the most densely populated area in Sweden, and it consists of farmland interspersed with hills, woodland, and lakes. It includes the Swedish capital, Stockholm. The southernmost region of Sweden, Götaland, is made up of dense forests and farmland and includes Lake Vänern and Lake Vättern. Skåne, in Sweden's far south, has the richest agricultural land in the country.

Focus on: A Landscape Shaped by Ice

Sweden's landscape was shaped by the ice that covered its territory thousands of years ago. The weight and movement of these great ice sheets created smooth-sided valleys and deep lakes. It also sculpted the distinctive shapes of the Kölen Mountains. Fast-moving glacial rivers deposited sand and silt to form the fertile soils of Sweden's central plains. Today, small glaciers remain on many mountains in the country's far north.

▶ A farm on the edge of Lake Vättern. This lake—the second largest in Sweden, after Vänern—is noted for its clean water.

SWEDEN'S CLIMATE

Sweden enjoys a warmer climate than its northern location might suggest. This is because of the warming effect of the Gulf Stream, an ocean current that flows in the Atlantic Ocean northward from the Equator and brings mild, wet weather to Sweden's southwestern coast. Generally, the weather in Sweden can be quite changeable, with sunshine and rain following in quick succession.

Sweden's long length means that its climate differs from north to south. This difference is most marked in the winter, when the north can be blanketed in thick snow while the south experiences rainfall. The average minimum temperature for January in Göteborg, on

Sweden's west coast, is 26.6 °Fahrenheit (-3 °Celsius). In Piteå in the north on the Gulf of Bothnia it is 8.6 °F (-13 °C) and has been known to drop to -36.4 °F (-38 °C). Snow starts to fall in the north as early as September and stays on the ground until April or May, when spring finally arrives. The waters of the Gulf of Bothnia freeze every winter. In central Sweden,

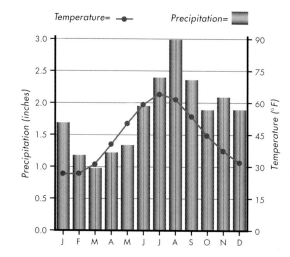

▲ Average monthly climate conditions in Stockholm

▼ A winter landscape in Södermanland, located in eastern Sweden. Winters can be long and very cold in parts of Sweden.

the snows come later and melt sooner, while the south of Sweden is often snow-free all winter. The waters around southern Sweden very rarely freeze.

SUMMERTIME

Sweden's summer lasts from mid June to mid August. Differences between the north and the south are far less marked during these months because of the long days in the north, which raise temperatures. As a result, in both Piteå and Göteborg, the average maximum temperature in July is 69.8 °F (21 °C).

 Did You Know?

The temperature is below freezing for an average of 71 days per year in Malmö, located in southern Sweden. In Haparanda, which is near the Arctic Circle in northern Sweden, the temperature remains below freezing for an average of 184 days per year.

Focus on: Sweden's Forests

More than half of Sweden's land area is covered with trees—deciduous forests in the south and coniferous forests in the north. Deciduous trees such as beech, oak, elm, ash, and lime grow in the southernmost regions. In the springtime the floors of these forests are covered in wild flowers. Further north, spruce and pine are the main coniferous trees. In the mountainous regions, the hardy birch, a deciduous tree, grows at higher altitudes than the coniferous forest. Beneath the birch trees, woody shrubs such as crowberry, bilberry, and whortleberry flourish. Picking edible berries and finding edible fungi are popular weekend pastimes among Swedes in late summer and early fall.

▼ A man and his young son check a mushroom guidebook as they gather wild mushrooms in a forest close to Skokloster, in the Uppland area.

CHAPTER 4

Population and Settlements

Sweden has a population of 9 million people. Up until the middle of the twentieth century, this population was almost entirely made up of native-born Swedes, with small Finnish and Sami minorities. Since World War II, however, there has been steady immigration into Sweden from countries all over the world. The arrival of immigrants into the country has raised many issues about how these "new Swedes" should be integrated into Swedish society.

IMMIGRATION AND EMIGRATION

Although Sweden has a long history of people settling within its borders—for example, the German Hansa merchants of the thirteenth and fourteenth centuries—immigration was not sufficiently large scale to have any significant effect on the country's population structure until the twentieth century . The waves of emigration in the late nineteenth and early twentieth centuries, however, did have an effect. The loss of 1.5 million people from a population of between 4 and 5 million led to labor shortages when the Swedish economy began to expand in the 1950s. Refugees from surrounding countries made up the first wave of Sweden's immigrants during World War II. They were followed in the 1950s and 1960s by people from countries such as Finland, the former Yugoslavia, Greece, Italy, Turkey, and Poland. Most of these people came to Sweden to find work.

▼ People on a street in Göteborg, on the west coast of Sweden. Göteborg has a large number of immigrant residents. Immigrants make up roughly 20 percent of the city's population.

During the 1970s, the demand for labor in Sweden decreased. The Swedish government placed restrictions on immigration, and the number of people coming to Sweden fell.

Since the 1980s, however, Sweden has been generous in its provision of sanctuary for large numbers of refugees and asylum seekers, including Kurds from Turkey and Iran and people from Iraq, Chile, and the former Yugoslavia. Today, foreign-born or first-generation immigrants make up about 10 percent of Sweden's population.

Population Data

- Population: 9 million
- Population 0–14 yrs: 17%
- Population 15–64 yrs: 65%
- Population 65+ yrs: 18%
- Population growth rate: 0.3%
- Population density: 51.8 per sq mile/ 20 per sq km
- Urban population: 83%
- Major cities:
  Stockholm 1,729,000
  Göteborg   829,000

Source: United Nations and World Bank

Focus on: Sami Life

The Sami live in a region known as Sápmi, or Lapland, that extends across northern Sweden, Norway, Finland, and Russia. It is estimated that there are between 70,000 and 80,000 Sami, and that between 17,000 and 20,000 of them live in Sweden. Traditional Sami occupations were reindeer herding, hunting, fishing, and farming. Today, only a small number of Sami continue to herd reindeer, but the animal remains very important in Sami culture. Many Sami work in tourism, mining, fishing, or farming. They have their own language, music, and artistic traditions, many of which can be experienced at the famous market and festival which is held in Jokkmokk, in northern Sweden, every February.

▼ Sami in a traditional *kata* (hut). In Arvidsjaur, which is located in Norrland, a complete Sami village has been preserved.

A MULTICULTURAL SOCIETY?

When immigrants first began to arrive in Sweden, it was presumed that these people would adopt the language and customs of their new country and become Swedes. In the 1970s, Sweden's government revised these ideas and set out new guidelines under three headings: equality, freedom of cultural choice, and cooperation and solidarity. The aim was to give immigrants equal rights with the rest of Sweden's population; to allow them to choose how far they wished to adopt Swedish customs; and to work together to resolve problems.

Since the 1980s, however, Sweden has struggled to cope with the number of people seeking refuge within its borders. Problems with the country's economy have led to high unemployment, resulting in many immigrants being unable to get jobs and relying on Sweden's welfare system to survive. Tensions between different communities have erupted in racist attacks, such as the ones that occurred in 1993 in Trollhättan, near Göteborg in western Sweden, when two Somali immigrants were badly beaten and the local mosque was burned down. In reaction to those attacks, the municipal council in Trollhättan has worked hard to resolve its problems through improved education, better facilities for its immigrant population, and a zero-tolerance approach to racism.

WHERE DO PEOPLE LIVE?

Sweden has a very low population density and large areas of the country are uninhabited. The average population density for the whole country is 51.8 people per sq mile (20 per sq km). There is, however, a wide range of population densities around the country—from about 650 people per sq mile (253 per sq km) in Stockholm to only about 8 people per sq mile (3 per sq km) in Norrbotten, the most northern of Sweden's counties. Eighty-three percent of Sweden's population lives in cities, with only 17 percent living in the countryside. Most of the country's population is centered in the south, particularly around the large metropolitan areas of Stockholm, Göteborg, and Malmö. Many

▼ A Turkish woman at work in the kitchen of a restaurant in Rinkeby, a suburb of Stockholm with a very large immigrant population.

immigrants and their children have found themselves living on the outskirts of Sweden's major cities, often in communities with other immigrants, leading to fears about racial segregation and discrimination.

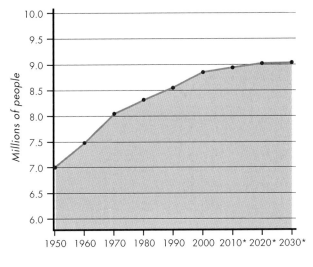

* Projected population

▲ Population growth, 1950–2030

Focus on: Stockholm

Sweden's capital, Stockholm, lies on the country's eastern coast. Known as the "city that floats on water," the central part of this beautiful city is built on 14 islands where Lake Mälaren meets the Saltsjön (Salt Sea) on the Baltic coast. The population of Stockholm municipality is 765,000, while the greater urban area that forms the metropolitan area of Stockholm has a population of 1,729,000. It the largest city in Scandinavia. A large number of foreign citizens, including Finns, Iranians, Iraqis, Chileans, and Turks, are permanent residents of Stockholm. There are many local programs to help these immigrant populations feel at home in Swedish society. For example, the Livstycket Association, which is based in a district of Stockholm with a large immigrant population, encourages people to create textile art and clothing while at the same time helping them learn to speak Swedish.

▶ A wooden house in Sweden's countryside. Many houses in Sweden are made out of wood, because it is a plentiful resource in the country. The color this house is painted—called Falun red—is a popular choice for wooden houses in Sweden.

CHAPTER 5

Government and Politics

Sweden is a democratic country, with an elected parliament and a hereditary monarchy. Its present king, Carl XVI Gustaf, came to the throne in 1973. He is a descendant of one of Napoleon Bonaparte's marshals, Jean Baptiste Bernadotte. Bernadotte was elected to be the Swedish king in 1810 and was crowned in 1818 as King Karl XIV Johan. The heir to the throne is the king's eldest daughter, Crown Princess Victoria. This is in line with the Act of Succession adopted in 1980 that gave the right of succession to the eldest child of the monarch, whether male or female. Before this, male children held precedence over female children.

▼ The Swedish Riksdagshuset, or parliament building, in Stockholm. The building lies on a small island in the city called Helgeandsholmen.

SWEDEN'S PARLIAMENT

"All public power in Sweden comes from the people." This is the first sentence of Sweden's constitution, and it reflects the importance of a democratic and egalitarian society to the Swedish people. Sweden's parliament is called the Riksdag, and it has 349 members. These members of parliament (MPs) are elected every four years in general elections. Every Swedish citizen 18 years old or over has the right to vote, and participation in general elections is usually high. In the 2002 election, 80.1 percent of the voting population cast votes.

The Riksdag appoints a prime minister who then chooses ministers to lead the various departments covering areas such as defense, agriculture, foreign affairs, health, justice, and

sustainable development. Together, the prime minister (who, since 1996, has been the Social Democrat Göran Persson) and his or her ministers form the government of Sweden.

POLITICAL PARTIES

Today, seven political parties are represented in the Riksdag: the Social Democrats, the Moderates, the Liberals, the Christian Democrats, the Center Party, the Left Party, and the Green Party. The Social Democrats are Sweden's largest political party, and the party has governed the country almost continuously since the 1930s (except for 1976–1982 and 1991–1994). Sweden's political parties can be categorized as socialist (Social Democrat, Left, and Green parties) or nonsocialist (Moderate, Liberal, Center, and Christian Democrat parties). Sweden's political system operates largely on the principle of consensus, with different parties often working together to achieve a common aim.

Focus on: Neo-Nazis in Sweden

In 1999, the murder of a trade union activist named Björn Söderberg was just one of several fatal incidents involving neo-Nazi groups that sparked nationwide rallies to protest increasing neo-Nazi violence. According to a 2001 report published by Sweden's government, the growth of extreme racist groups in Sweden and abroad—known as "white power" groups—has been helped by the ease of communication and anonymity offered by the Internet.

 Did You Know?

Women are well represented in Sweden's parliament. Female MPs made up 45.3 percent of the Riksdag after the 2002 election.

▼ Inside the Riksdagshuset, members of Sweden's parliament sit in the main chamber.

LOCAL GOVERNMENT

Sweden is divided into 21 regions, or counties, and 290 municipalities. Elections for county and municipal councils occur every four years, at the same time as the country's general elections. Foreign nationals who have lived in Sweden for three years or more may vote in county and municipal elections, although they are not permitted to vote in general elections. County councils are responsible for health care in their regions. They also promote regional growth by supporting local businesses. Municipal councils provide education, child care, and care for the elderly; they also are responsible for a wide range of services including housing, emergency services, water, waste management, energy, and cultural and recreational facilities. These services are funded through local income taxes that are set by the municipal and county councils and which average about 30 percent of taxable income. In recent years, many of Sweden's municipal councils have also taken responsibility for increasing numbers of refugee inhabitants. They are given special funds directly from the national government for this purpose.

SWEDEN AND THE EUROPEAN UNION

Sweden became a member of the European Union (EU) in 1995 after a referendum (national vote). This vote showed that many Swedes were uncertain about becoming more closely linked with their European neighbors: 52.3 percent of Swedes voted for joining the EU, but 46.8 percent voted against it. In 1999, the EU introduced a common currency, the euro, in 11 of its 15 member countries. Sweden was one of the countries that decided not to

▼ "Vote no" ("Rösta nej") reads this banner in the run-up to Sweden's 1994 referendum on whether the country should become a member of the European Union.

take part. In 2003, this decision was finalized by another referendum in which 55.9 percent of Swedes rejected the euro. Differences of opinion about the EU have had an effect on national politics. The Left Party led the campaign against the euro. The Social Democrats were divided over the issue, although the party officially supported the failed campaign in favor of the euro.

TAXES AND THE WELFARE STATE

Sweden is renowned for its welfare system, which is paid for by the highest taxes of any country in the world. Swedes pay an average local tax of between 29 and 34 percent. Higher earners pay an additional national tax of 20 percent. The aim of Sweden's high taxes has been to redistribute income so that all members of society in the country have equal access to education, health care, child care, and other services. Since the 1980s, however, Sweden has struggled to cope with the increased demands on its welfare system, and funding has decreased as a result of the economic crisis of the early 1990s. Nevertheless, Sweden's welfare system remains

an important part of Swedish society and one that many Swedes prize very highly.

 Did You Know?

A high proportion of Sweden's GDP is made up of tax revenues. In 2003, Sweden's figure was 50.7 percent, compared with 35.6 percent in Britain and 25.6 percent in the United States.

Focus on: The Sami Parliament

In 1993, King Carl XVI Gustaf opened the first Sami parliament in Kiruna, which is located in northern Sweden. The Sami parliament decides how to distribute money from the Swedish government to Sami organizations. It also deals with matters such as land use, fishing, and hunting, which are of great importance to the Sami people. The Sami Parliament is also involved in the management of Sami schools.

▶ A care-staff member talks to three residents of a state-run home for the elderly in Stockholm. State-funded care for children and for older people is given a high priority in Sweden.

CHAPTER 6

Energy and Resources

Sweden has no oil or coal reserves. It, therefore, imports all of the oil it needs for energy production and other uses. However, the country does have huge potential for renewable energy, including water power, wind power, and the burning of biofuels. These energy sources are playing an increasingly important part in the country's energy policy. Sweden has large mineral reserves—including deposits of iron ore, copper, and silver—and these form the basis for a large sector of the country's economy.

HYDROELECTRIC POWER

Sweden has been making use of its many rivers to produce electricity since the 1880s, and its use of hydroelectric power (HEP) has expanded rapidly since the 1930s. In the 1960s, concern about the environmental effects of constructing dams led to a government decision not to build any hydropower facilities on the four major undammed rivers in northern Sweden, although hydroelectric plants continued to be used and developed elsewhere. Today, hydroelectric power continues to play an important part in Sweden's mix of energy resources, producing 45.6 percent of the country's electricity.

NUCLEAR POWER

Before the 1970s, Sweden relied almost entirely on HEP and imported oil for its energy requirements. The oil crisis in the 1970s—during which oil prices rose rapidly and oil supplies from the Middle East were cut off to many countries—led Sweden's government to turn to nuclear power for electricity generation.

▼ Felled tree trunks are stacked onto a trailer in Sundsvall. In Sweden, biofuels produced from the wastes from timber processing are an increasingly important energy resource.

Six nuclear power stations were opened in Sweden in the 1970s, and another six in the 1980s. But, after a referendum held in 1980, Sweden's government decided to close down its nuclear power stations by 2010 if alternative energy sources could be found and relied upon. The Chernobyl disaster in 1986, which badly affected Sweden, reinforced public concern about the dangers of nuclear power. The biggest advantage of nuclear power, however, is that it does not put out carbon dioxide (CO_2) emissions, the so-called "greenhouse gases." Today, 46.3 percent of Sweden's electricity is still produced by nuclear power. Because the country gives high priority to reducing CO_2 emissions, public opinion is largely in favor of continuing to use the existing nuclear reactors until they can no longer be used. Nevertheless, the government is still planning to phase out nuclear power.

Focus on: Chernobyl

In April 1986, a huge explosion at a nuclear power plant in the Soviet Union sent radioactive material into the atmosphere across much of northern Europe. The north of Sweden was badly hit by the fallout, particularly because large amounts of radioactive material were distributed by heavy rains that fell in the days following the Chernobyl explosion. Studies of the affected areas have linked a rise in the number of people suffering from various forms of cancer with the increased radiation exposure.

Energy Data

- Energy consumption as % of world total: 0.5%
- Energy consumption by sector (% of total),
  Industry: 35.9
  Transportation: 23.0
  Agriculture: 1.4
  Services: 13.7
  Residential: 22.6
  Other: 3.4
- CO_2 emissions as % of world total: 0.2
- CO_2 emissions per capita in tons per year: 6

Source: World Resources Institute

▼ The Barsebäck nuclear power station, located in southern Sweden, was built in the 1960s. It was fully closed down in 2005.

▲ A wind turbine near the village of Simrishamn in the region of Skåne. In the future, increasing amounts of energy in Sweden will be produced by wind power.

RENEWABLE ENERGY

In an effort to replace nuclear power, the government of Sweden is investing heavily in renewable forms of energy. Sweden is one of the world leaders in the use of biofuels as an energy source. Biofuels are fuels that are produced from organic matter. In Sweden, they consist mostly of wastes from timber processing, such as wood chips and sawdust. This waste is burned to produce electricity and generate heat. In some of Sweden's cities, biofuels provide the heat for district heating systems. In these systems, hot water is pumped through pipes to provide heating and hot water supplies for all the homes and businesses in a particular area. In the southern city of Lund, the district heating system is fueled by geothermal energy. There, hot water is pumped from deep below Earth's surface (11,483 ft/3,500 m), and, once the heat energy has been used, is then pumped back into the ground. This project has significantly reduced the use of oil in the city, and therefore has also reduced CO_2 emissions.

Wind power is another potential energy source that Sweden's government plans to exploit further in the future. There are plans for new wind farms along the coast and around Lake Vänern. Plans also exist for an offshore wind farm in the Öresund sea strait, between southern Sweden and Denmark.

NATURAL RESOURCES

Sweden is the largest producer of iron ore in the European Union, and it is a major iron ore exporter. It is also a leading producer of other metals, such as copper, lead, zinc, silver, and gold. The mining industry is based in the north of the country, and exploration for new reserves is ongoing, with new mines continuing to open. Sweden has made use of its mineral resources to become a major producer of high-quality iron and steel. The country's steel industry is highly modernized. Computers are used to make every part of the process as efficient as possible, and steps are taken to minimize impact on the environment. Sweden's steel industry uses less energy and puts out fewer emissions than similar industries in other countries.

Timber is another major resource in Sweden. Forests cover about three-quarters of the country, and timber and related products make up about 12 percent of Sweden's export income. Timber is used for building and for the manufacture of furniture and other items. The byproducts of these timber-consuming industries provide an important source of biofuels.

Sweden's long coastline and easy access to the sea mean that fish has always played an important part in the national diet. Today, the country's fishing industry employs about 4,000 people, about half of whom work on boats catching fish. Another 1,800 people work in the fish processing industry and another 300 in aquaculture, or fish farming. The bulk of Sweden's catch is made up of cod, herring, sprat, and prawns. Sweden's inland waters—particularly the large southern lakes of Vänern,

Hjälmaren, Mälaren, and Vättern—are also an important source of fish such as pike, perch, and vendace. Although fishing plays an important role in the local economy in many places, it is a relatively small industry in the country, accounting for just 0.2 percent of its GDP.

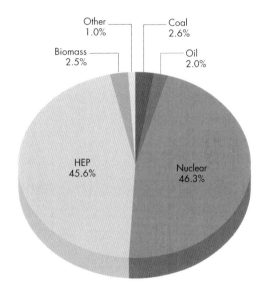

▲ Electricity production by type

▼ A fishing boat is surrounded by seagulls off Bohuslän, on the west coast of Sweden. There are many fishing villages along this rugged coastline.

CHAPTER 7

Economy and Income

During the twentieth century, Sweden rapidly transformed itself from an agricultural country to an industrial one. It based its industrialization on its natural resources—iron ore, timber, and plentiful HEP to provide energy. However, because of its relatively small home market, many Swedish companies have always looked abroad to sell their products. This early emphasis on exporting and globalization has resulted in the growth of a large number of multinational companies that have their roots in Sweden, including household names such as Volvo, Saab, Ikea, Ericsson, H&M, and Electrolux.

ECONOMIC CRISIS AND RECOVERY

The development of Sweden's industries throughout much of the twentieth century resulted in steady economic growth. In the early 1990s, however, this growth was interrupted as the country entered a period of economic crisis.

An international recession led to a reduction in demand for Swedish products and a corresponding drop in manufacturing output. Unemployment rose rapidly to 8 percent from an average of 2 or 3 percent throughout the 1980s. Low levels of manufacturing output, high levels of unemployment, population growth partly resulting from immigration, and the demands of the welfare state left the Swedish government struggling to cope. In 1993, Sweden's budget deficit (the amount by

? Did You Know?

Agriculture employs only 2 percent of the labor force in Sweden, and only 7 percent of the country's land is suitable for farming.

▼ An iron smelter in Falun, a mining area in central Sweden in the county of Dalarnas. Falun is famous for its red paint, which is traditionally produced from the waste products of its copper mines.

which a government's spending exceeds its income) rose to 12 percent of the country's GDP, the highest figure for any industrialized nation that year.

Cutbacks in spending on its welfare system and increased demand for the country's exports helped Sweden's economy begin to recover in 1994. Industrial production increased throughout the remainder of the 1990s. However, there was a shift in emphasis away from traditional industries, such as steel and timber, toward more high-tech sectors, such as telecommunications and information technology (IT), in which many of Sweden's companies are world leaders. By 1998, the budget deficit had turned into a budget surplus, and, by 2000, unemployment had dropped to about 4 percent.

Economic Data

- Gross National Income (GNI) in U.S.$: 321,401,159,680
- World rank by GNI: 19
- GNI per capita in U.S.$: 35,770
- World rank by GNI per capita: 10
- Economic growth: 3.6%

Source: World Bank

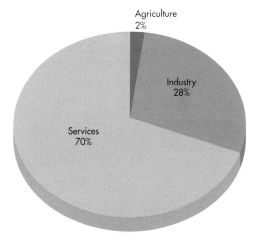

▲ Contribution by sector to national income

Focus on: Tetra Pak

In 1950, Swedish entrepreneur Dr. Ruben Rausing founded the first packaging company. In 1952, his company launched its first product—Tetra Classic—a tetrahedron-shaped (four-sided) carton made from plastic-coated cardboard that was used for storing and transporting milk and cream. Rausing had been working on this revolutionary packaging since 1943. Today, Tetra Pak is a multinational company with more than 20,000 employees worldwide, although the business is still owned by the Rausing family. Tetra Pak continues to innovate, with products such as Tetra Recart, which allows foods that are usually packaged in metal cans and glass jars to be packaged in square-shaped cartons. Tetra Recart was launched in the United States in 2004.

▲ A worker in a Volvo truck factory in Göteborg. Volvo is an important employer in the city.

RESEARCH AND DEVELOPMENT

Sweden has become known as a world leader in innovation, research, and design. Research-and-development spending is particularly high in Sweden's telecommunications, pharmaceutical, and transportation equipment companies. The importance of these sectors is reflected in the country's export statistics. Chemical products (which include pharmaceuticals) make up 12.1 percent of the total value of Sweden's exports, while electric and electronic equipment make up 15.5 percent, and transportation equipment makes up 15.2 percent. Although a high proportion of research work in the country is carried out by the multinational companies that are based in Sweden, Sweden's government has for many years emphasized the importance of development and innovation by funding research departments in Sweden's universities. It has also set up several councils that undertake research in various fields, including social sciences, medicine, engineering sciences, and education.

▼ This terminal in Stockholm handles the shipping of containers and bulk cargo.

WORKING IN SWEDEN

A large proportion of Sweden's workforce is employed by the public sector in fields such as education, medical care, child care, and care for the elderly. In 1990, 41 percent of Sweden's workforce was employed by the country's national government, municipal councils, and county councils. After cutbacks during the economic crisis, this figure fell to 34 percent by 2001. Many services that were under the control of Sweden's government have been opened up to competition, including the postal service, railways, and electricity supply. Reduction of state control has helped to boost economic growth and create more jobs in the country's private sector.

Relations between managers and employees have traditionally been good in Sweden. A large number of Sweden's employees are members of trade unions, which are a powerful force in the country. Decisions about pay increases and working conditions are made through collective bargaining, rather than being imposed by the government. Collective bargaining is nationwide negotiation between

union representatives and employers. Sweden's companies tends to be less hierarchical than in many other countries, with smaller differences in pay between managers and their employees and an emphasis on teamwork and agreement within a company. However, there is concern about the number of highly qualified young Swedes who choose to go abroad to work in countries such as the United States, where they can earn more money than they can in Sweden.

 Did You Know?

About 47 percent of Sweden's population belongs to the country's workforce.

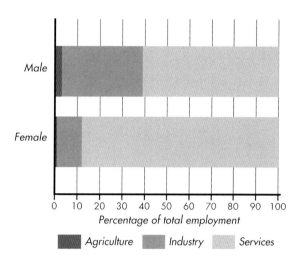

Percentage of total employment

- Agriculture
- Industry
- Services

▲ Labor force by sector and gender

Focus on: Women and Child Care

Since the 1960s, Sweden's government has put policies in place to encourage women to work. In particular, Sweden has an extensive network of nurseries and preschools, which allows parents to work full-time if they choose. The cost of child care is largely paid by revenue from taxes, but parents also pay a fee that is based on their income. Parents in Sweden are entitled to a generous amount of parental leave—480 days of leave can be taken by either parent—when a child is born.

◄ Children sit at a table with a caregiver and eat cereal in a nursery in Stockholm. This day-care center is funded and run by the government.

CHAPTER 8

Global Connections

Since the beginning of its history, Sweden has been a trading nation, with links across Europe. Today, Sweden's trading links are worldwide, as Sweden exports a large proportion of the goods and services made within its borders. Sweden also plays an important role in international organizations such as the United Nations (UN) and the European Union (EU), which it joined in 1995.

SWEDEN AND NEUTRALITY

Since the early nineteenth century, Sweden has had a policy of neutrality in armed conflicts. This policy was adopted after the Napoleonic Wars, during which Sweden lost much of its empire. In the twentieth century, Sweden maintained its neutrality throughout World War I and World War II. Sweden could not, however, remain untouched by events in Europe during these wars. When the Soviet Union attacked Finland in 1939, thousands of Swedes went to help the Finns in the fight against the Red (Soviet) Army. Later, after Germany had invaded and occupied Denmark and Norway, Sweden allowed unarmed German troops to travel through its territories to and from Norway. Sweden's policy of neutrality did not prevent it from building up its own armed forces so that it could defend itself in case of attack. Today, the defense industry is an important sector in Sweden's economy, with companies such as BAE Systems, Saab, and Ericsson involved in the manufacture and export of armaments and defense systems.

▼ Cranes are used to load ships at the docks in Göteborg. The city has long been a center of trade and commerce, and its port is the largest in Scandinavia.

NATO INVOLVEMENT

After the end of World War II, Norway and Denmark became members of the North Atlantic Treaty Organization (NATO). NATO was set up in 1949 to "promote stability and well-being in the North Atlantic area." Sweden remained outside NATO, preferring to continue with its policy of "non-participation in alliances in time of peace, aiming at neutrality in the event of war." In the 1990s, however, Sweden became a member of NATO's Partnership for Peace (PfP) and the Europe-Atlantic Partnership Council (EAPC). The PfP was set up in 1994 after the break-up of the Soviet Union and the end of the Cold War. An aim of the PfP is to promote cooperation between countries over security and defense. The EAPC, set up in 1997, offers an opportunity for regular meetings between representatives from more than 40 countries to discuss matters such as international crisis management and emergency planning.

 Did You Know?

Sixty percent of all goods produced in Sweden are exported.

▶ A Swedish Air Force pilot flies alongside a Saab 105 training jet. Saab manufactures a wide variety products for both military and civilian markets.

Focus on: Raoul Wallenberg

Raoul Wallenberg (1912–1947) came from one of Sweden's wealthiest and most influential families. He is famous for saving the lives of thousands of Jews during World War II. In 1944, Germany invaded the lands of its former ally, Hungary. The Germans immediately began to deport Hungarian Jews to concentration camps in occupied Poland. Wallenberg went to Hungary's capital, Budapest, to try to save them. Through a mixture of diplomacy, bribes, and threats he managed to set up safe houses in the city, where Jews could take refuge. Wallenberg declared these houses to be Swedish territory, which meant that Jews were protected from arrest there. It is estimated that Wallenberg rescued about 100,000 Jews. In 1944, the Soviet army invaded Hungary, and Wallenberg disappeared into captivity. The Soviets claim that he died in 1947, but his family does not know exactly what happened to him.

PEACEMAKERS

Sweden has produced some notable peacemakers and negotiators who have played major roles on the world stage. They include Folke Bernadotte, who worked for the United Nations in Palestine before his assassination in 1948, and Dag Hammarskjöld. Becoming Secretary General of the United Nations in 1953, Hammarskjöld used his diplomatic skills to good effect at moments of international tension ranging from the Korean War (1950–1953) to the Suez Crisis (1956). In 1961, he died in a plane crash on a UN mission to the Congo in Africa.

Sweden became a member of the UN in 1946. The UN is an important part of Swedish foreign policy, because it is seen as an organization through which smaller countries can play an important role towards world peace. Sweden has sent troops to many trouble spots around the world, including Kosovo and Bosnia, as part of UN peacekeeping operations. It has also provided high-profile negotiators such as Carl Bildt and Hans Blix. Bildt, who was prime minister of Sweden from 1991 to 1994, oversaw the reconstruction of Bosnia-Herzegovina after the civil war in the early 1990s. From 2000 to 2003, Blix headed the UN Monitoring, Verification, and Inspection Commission (UNMOVIC), which was in charge of monitoring the disarmament of Iraq's weapons of mass destruction. Blix has criticized both the United States and Britain for the decision to invade Iraq in 2003.

SWEDEN AND THE EU

Since it became a member of the European Union in 1995, Sweden has supported its enlargement. In 2004, the EU welcomed ten new members into the Union, including the Baltic states of Estonia, Lithuania, and Latvia. The Baltic states are of particular importance to Sweden, because they are close neighbors. Sweden's banks and companies have invested heavily in the economies of the Baltic states, and their membership in the EU will make trade and regional cooperation easier.

▼ The World Trade Center in Stockholm is a conference and exhibition center.

Focus on: The Nobel Prize

Alfred Nobel was born in Stockholm in 1833. His father was an engineer, and Alfred followed in his footsteps, studying chemical engineering in Sweden, Germany, France, and the United States. After years of dangerous experimentation—in the course of which his brother was killed during an experiment—Nobel developed an explosive material that he called dynamite. Dynamite revolutionized construction work, making it easier to drill tunnels and dig canals. Nobel quickly became a rich man and founded factories in more than 20 countries. When he died in 1896, Nobel's will stated that his inheritance was to be used for annual prizes to acknowledge great achievements in physics, chemistry, medicine, literature, and peace. The awarding of these prestigious prizes—the Nobel Prizes—continues to this day, with the award ceremony held in the Concert Hall in Stockholm, followed by a banquet in the City Hall.

▲ At the 2002 ceremony in Stockholm, Masatoshi Koshiba (left) received the Nobel Prize in Physics, and Koichi Tanaka (right) received the Nobel Prize in Chemistry. Nobel Prize winners receive a medal, a personal diploma, and prize money.

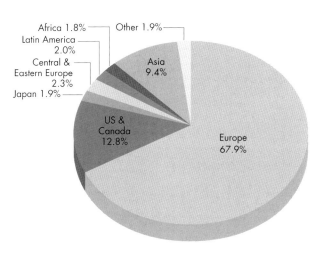

▲ Destination of exports by major trading region

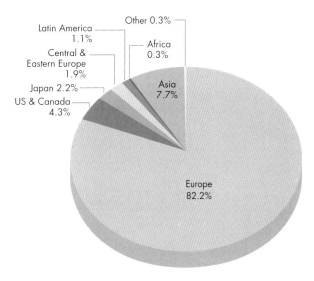

▲ Origin of imports by major trading region

CHAPTER 9

Transportation and Communications

Sweden is a sparsely populated country. Distances between settlements in the north of the country can be huge. For this reason, good communications and infrastructure have been vital to Sweden's development. Today, the country has an extensive road system, with well-built and maintained roads even in remote areas. It also has extensive ferry, railway, and air links.

ROAD AND RAIL

Sweden has 132,505 miles (213,237 km) of roads. Car ownership in the country is high, at 452 per 1,000 people. Most families own at least one car. Roads and bridges in Sweden are all toll free, with the exception of the Öresund Link, which connects Malmö and Copenhagen, the capital of Denmark. Sweden also has state-run car ferries, which transport vehicles across short stretches of water in some places.

The country's rail network reaches from the border with Norway, in the north, to Sweden's southernmost tip. The state-owned railway company Statens Järnvägar (SJ) operates most of Sweden's long distance train routes, but private companies such as Connex and Tågkompaniet also operate some train services. A high-speed "tilting" train known as the X2000 was developed in the 1980s to cope with the curves of many sections of track on Sweden's railways. While high-speed trains in France and Japan run on almost straight, specially built track, Swedish engineers used tilting technology to allow the trains to run at high speeds around bends. The X2000 was introduced in 1990. It has reduced the time of a rail journey from Stockholm to Göteborg by one hour. Stockholm is the only Swedish city with an underground railway system.

◀ A bus waits to meet a ferry service from Stockholm that serves the islands and coastal region around the city. Sweden is well known for such integrated transportation planning.

The Tunnelbanan, or T-banan, has three lines and about 68 miles (110 km) of track. Göteborg has an extensive and modern tram system linking the center of the city with its suburbs.

AIR TRAVEL

Stockholm's main international airport is Arlanda. It is located about 25 miles (40 km) north of the city center. Budget airlines are increasingly using the smaller Skavsta and Västerås Airports, which lie about 62 miles (100 km) south and east of Stockholm, respectively. Most domestic flights use Bromma Airport, which is closest to Stockholm's center. Göteborg and Malmö also have their own airports. Flying is an important means of getting around Sweden. A variety of low-cost airlines, such as Skyways and Sverigeflyg, provide flights.

Transport & Communications Data

- Total roads: 132,505 miles/213,237 km
- Total paved roads: 104,149 miles/ 167,604 km
- Total unpaved roads: 28,356 miles/ 45,633 km
- Total railways: 7,134 miles/11,481 km
- Airports: 254
- Cars per 1,000 people: 452
- Cellular phones per 1,000 people: 1,034
- Personal computers per 1,000 people: 621.3
- Internet users per 1,000 people: 756

Source: World Bank and CIA World Factbook

Focus on: The Öresund Link

Copenhagen, Denmark's capital, and Malmö, in Sweden, are separated by a nearly 9-mile (14-km) channel called the Öresund. Debate about building a link between the two cities began in the nineteenth century. The project became reality when work on it started in the 1990s. The Öresund Link, which opened in 2000, is a mixture of an 5-mile (8-km) bridge, a 2.5-mile (4-km) artificial island, and a 2.5-mile (4-km) tunnel. It has two levels, with a road on the upper deck and a railway line running below it.

▲ The spectacular Öresund Link spans the 9-mile (14-km) channel between Malmö and Copenhagen.

TRANSPORTATION BY WATER

Ferries provide sea links between Sweden and other countries including Britain, Germany, Denmark, Finland, Estonia, and Poland. Stockholm, Malmö, and Göteborg are all major ports. Sweden also has an extensive network of canals. The most famous of these is the Göta Canal, which was built in the nineteenth century to connect Sweden's west coast with the Baltic Sea. The canal extends about 360 miles (579 km) from Göteborg in the west, linking Lake Vänern and Lake Vättern. It was originally used for transporting timber and iron, but today it is a popular tourist attraction.

COMMUNICATIONS

Sweden is a world leader in communications and information technology. This is reflected in the number of cellular phones in the country and use of the Internet among its people. According to Telekom Online, Sweden has more cellular phones than it has people—10 million cell phones for a population of 9 million people. This does not mean that every person in Sweden owns a cell phone; rather, many people in the country own more than one cell phone. In 2005, Sweden became the first country in the world to introduce a secure system of electronic identification using cellular phones. Called e-ID, this system will allow people to access their bank accounts and other secure information via their phones.

An extremely high proportion of people in Sweden use the Internet—75.6 percent in 2005 compared to 63 percent for the United States and 62.8 percent in Britain. Many Swedes use the Internet regularly for shopping, looking for jobs, reading online newspapers, and booking tickets. Government agencies in Sweden, such as county and municipal councils and the tax board, have highly developed Web sites that allow people to contact

◀ Workers making electronic components in a Stockholm laboratory owned by Ericsson, the Swedish electronics and communications company.

them via the Internet. Sweden's government Web sites are set up so that its people can, for example, submit their tax returns online.

MEDIA

Until 1987, Sweden's national public service broadcaster, Sveriges Television (SVT), provided the only television channels available in the country. Since that year, many commercial channels have been introduced, some of which are available only via cable or satellite. The country's next big media change will be in 2008, when analog television transmissions will end. Beginning in 2008, all TVs in the country be converted to digital, either through a box on top of the set or through cable or satellite connections. Sweden will be one of the first countries in Europe to make this change.

Newspapers and magazines are very popular in Sweden. About 90 percent of adults in Sweden read a newspaper every day, and many of them have a newspaper delivered to their home in the morning. The most popular national papers include *Dagens Nyheter* (The Daily News) and *Göteborgs-Posten* (The Göteborg Post). The country also has evening newspapers, which are published at about noon each day, and many smaller newspapers that target local readerships. Sweden was also the original home of *Metro*, which was launched in 1995 in Stockholm. This free newspaper is now distributed to commuters, office workers, and shoppers in 88 major cities around the world. It reaches about 18.5 million readers every day.

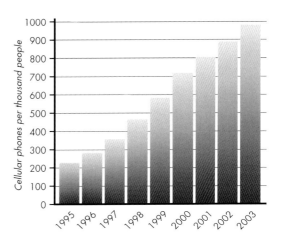

▲ Cellular phone use, 1995–2003

 Did You Know?

Swedish ports handled more than 185 million tons (168 million metric tons) of goods in 2004.

► The Kaknäs Television Tower in Stockholm stands 508 ft (155 m) tall, the tallest structure in Scandinavia. It is the center of radio and television broadcasts across Sweden.

CHAPTER 10

Education and Health

Sweden has extremely high standards of education and health care. The country allocates 7.7 percent of its GDP to education and 9.2 percent of its GDP to health care, putting it among the top spenders in these areas in the developed world. Sweden has one of the highest literacy rates in the world.

EARLY EDUCATION

Sweden has an extensive system of early education and child care to look after children before they start school. Children in Sweden start their compulsory schooling late compared to children in many other developed countries. Children in Sweden must attend school from the ages of 7 to 16, but preschool places are allocated to 6-year-old children whose parents wish them to attend at this age. The country's school year starts in mid to late August and finishes in mid June, with a vacation over the Christmas and New Year period. Most children go to the school that is nearest to their home. Public education is free, and it includes school meals, transportation to and from school, and equipment and books. Sweden has a few independent schools, many of which offer specializations—for example, sports or music—not emphasized in the public schools.

HIGHER EDUCATION AND BEYOND

The vast majority—about 98 percent— of Swedish students continue on to upper secondary school, which is also free. Students can choose subjects from 17 national programs, including both academic and vocational courses, that they study for three years. Many students in Sweden continue their studies at universities or colleges that specialize in areas such as teacher training or health care training. Tuition for higher education is free, and students can apply for government grants and loans to help with their living expenses. Sweden has universities in all of its major cities—Stockholm, Göteborg, Uppsala, and Lund—as well as specialized institutions such as the Karolinska Institute,

◀ Children at work during a question-and-answer session at a school in Sweden.

for medicine, and the Luleå University of Technology. The country also has several private higher-education institutions, including the Stockholm School of Economics and the Chalmers University of Technology.

Continued learning in adulthood is considered important in Sweden. Many people take courses at one of the 147 "folk high schools" around the country. Adult learning is financed by government grants. Municipalities are required by law to provide education for adults and to give adult learners the skills needed "to take part in social and working life." Similarly, municipalities must provide language classes for immigrants to learn and improve their basic Swedish.

Education and Health Data

- Life expectancy at birth, male: 77.9
- Life expectancy at birth, female: 82.4
- Infant mortality rate per 1,000: 3
- Under five mortality rate per 1,000: 3
- Physicians per 1,000 people: 3
- Health expenditure as % of GDP: 9.2%
- Education expenditure as % of GDP: 7.7%
- Primary net enrollment: 100%
- Student-teacher ratio, primary: 11.2
- Adult literacy as % age 15+: near 100%

Source: United Nations Agencies and World Bank

Focus on: Sami Schools

Children from Sami families in northern Sweden may, if they wish, attend Sami school. There are Sami schools in Karesuando, Lannavaara, Kiruna, Gällivare, Jokkmokk, and Tärnaby. These schools are funded by the state and take students between the ages of 7 and 12. Children in these schools are taught in the Sami language as well as Swedish, and the curriculum covers Sami culture and issues together with the subjects taught in other municipal schools. The schools are run by the Sami School Board, which is overseen by the Sami Parliament.

◀ University students wear their white graduation caps as they rush out to meet friends and relatives after their graduation ceremony in Uppsala in 2003.

Sweden has one of the lowest infant mortality rates (the number of babies who die at birth) in the world, at 3 per 1,000 births. It also has one of the world's highest life expectancies, at 77.9 years for men and 82.4 years for women. It has an efficient health service that is completely free for people up to the age of 20.

PAYING FOR HEALTH CARE

Sweden's health care system is run by the county councils. The health care system is financed through contributions made by employers and an income tax that is set by individual county councils. Patients also pay a fee when they consult a doctor, but once they have paid a certain amount (SEK 900, or U.S.$123) in a 12-month period, treatment is free. Similarly, patients must pay up to a certain amount for medications, but, after that amount is paid, their medications are subsidized.

A major issue in Sweden is the high rate of absence from work because of sickness, often as a result of stress-related problems. Swedes' average number of days taken off work because of illness has risen rapidly from 17 in 1995 to 32 in 2002. In 1993, the country's government changed the rules so that employees would lose their pay for the first sick day taken off work. After this initial "qualifying day," however, employees receive about 80 percent of their salary while they are off work. Many people at least partly attribute the high amount of sick leave taken in Sweden to this generous policy. In 2003, the cost of Sweden's sick-leave payments was SEK 110 billion, or U.S.$15 billion. The country's government is trying to encourage people to work, even on a part-time basis.

In general, Sweden's population has been growing steadily

◀ A doctor examines an elderly patient at a hospital in Stockholm. Sweden has a very high standard of health care.

healthier since the 1930s. Issues for the future include an increasing number of people with allergies and problems with obesity, particularly in young people. According to a study by Karolinska University Hospital, the number of obese 7-year-olds in Stockholm has increased from 8.5 percent to 21 percent since 1990. Experts blame a mixture of the increased popularity of fast foods and fizzy drinks and more hours spent in front of the television and computer screen. These problems are growing

in spite of Sweden's nationwide sports programs aimed at children and the fact that commercials aimed at children under 12 are banned on Swedish television.

Focus on: Winter Swedes

During the dark days of winter in Sweden, people in the country's north experience 24-hour darkness, while even in its south days are short and cold. Many Swedes travel abroad during the winter holiday season to find the Sun. Destinations such as Thailand and Sri Lanka are popular, as shown by the number of Swedish deaths when a giant tsunami devastated coastlines around the Indian Ocean in 2004. More than 500 Swedes were killed in the disaster—the highest number of people of any European nation.

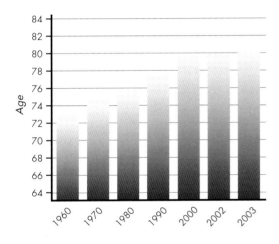

▲ Life expectancy at birth, 1960–2003

▼ The festival of St. Lucia, which is held in December, brightens up the long, dark days of winter for many Swedish people.

CHAPTER 11

Culture and Religion

Sweden occupies a central place in Europe's cultural traditions. It has given the world many famous writers, musicians, actors, and artists, including the playwright August Strindberg, the pop group ABBA, the actress Greta Garbo, the filmmaker Ingmar Bergman, and the artist Carl Larsson.

LANGUAGE

Although Swedish is the main language spoken in Sweden, it is not by law the country's official language. In 2005, a proposal to formalize the status of Swedish was narrowly rejected by the country's parliament. Nevertheless, Swedes are very proud of their language, which is related to Danish and Norwegian. Most Swedes also speak at least one other language; English is most common, but French, German, and Spanish are also popular. Sweden has five official minority languages: Sami (Lapp), Finnish, Meänkieli (Tornedalen Finnish), Yiddish, and Romani Chib (a Gypsy language). In recent years, a variety of Swedish has emerged from city suburbs that have large immigrant populations. This new language is a mixture of Swedish and words taken from the immigrants' home languages, and it is known as Rinkeby Swedish, after a suburb of Stockholm. Rinkeby Swedish varies according to the background and location of the people speaking it.

FOOD

In the days before refrigeration, the storage of food was vitally important for survival through the long winter months in Sweden. The summer harvest of fruits and vegetables was preserved and pickled; meat and fish were smoked, salted, or dried for storage. Today,

◀ This painting by Swedish artist Carl Larsson (1853–1919) was one of a series of paintings he made of his home in Sundborn. Larsson's work became hugely popular in Sweden and beyond.

modern methods of food storage have made such measures unnecessary, but the traditional tastes of Swedish food and the importance of seasonal produce remain very important. People still go out into the forests and wild places of Sweden to pick berries and mushrooms, and crayfish and fermented herring are national delicacies that are still valued and enjoyed. The best known Swedish meal is probably *smörgåsbord*—a buffet of many types of delicious food, including open sandwiches and appetizers, from which people help themselves.

Focus on: Runes

Runes are an ancient form of writing used in Sweden and other northern European countries. The runic alphabet takes its name, *futhark*, from its first six letters, which represent the sounds of *f, u, th, a, r,* and *k* (the *t* and the *h* are one letter). It was developed by early Germanic peoples. More than 3,000 stones inscribed with runes have been found in Sweden, many in the region around Uppsala. These stones were usually memorials to the dead. The runes were cut into them, then painted to make them more visible.

? Did You Know?

Ombudsman is a word that has come directly from the Swedish language into English. It means a person who works as an official who monitors public agencies and investigates complaints made by members of the public.

▼ The Swedish pop group ABBA became famous after winning the Eurovision Song Contest in 1974. They went on to become one of the most successful pop groups of all time.

THE ARTS

All aspects of the arts play an important part in Swedish life. Large amounts of public money are spent on subsidies to support cultural and artistic activities with the aim of making them available to everyone. Sweden's government funds some major institutions, including the Royal Opera and the Royal Dramatic Theater. Municipal and county councils allocate funds to museums, libraries, local theaters, orchestras, and opera and dance companies. Sweden's vibrant artistic, literary, and musical tradition continues to produce talents such as film director Lukas Moodysson (born 1969), and author Per Olov Enquist (b. 1934).

RELIGION IN SWEDEN

Until 2000, when the link between church and state was broken, the national church of Sweden was the Lutheran Church. Before then, a child born to a parent who belonged to the Church of Sweden automatically became a member. Now it is up to parents to decide whether or not to have their children baptized. Other Christian churches also have a presence in Sweden, notably the Roman Catholic Church, the Pentecostal Church, and various Baptist churches. As a result of immigration into Sweden, the country's Muslim population has increased rapidly to between 300,000 and 350,000 in 2004, and there are mosques being built in several places. There is a Jewish population of about 18,000 people.

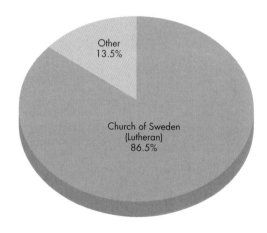

Other
13.5%

Church of Sweden
(Lutheran)
86.5%

▲ Major religions

 Did You Know?

The festival of Walpurgis is named after Saint Walburga, who was born in England in 710.

◀ A sculpture appears out of the waters of the Norrström, in Strömmen, which is located in the middle of Stockholm. The Royal Opera House is in the background.

FESTIVALS

Many of Sweden's major festivals—such as Advent, Christmas, and Easter—are based around the Christian calendar. Christmas is celebrated mainly on Christmas Eve, when children are given presents. At Easter, children dress up as witches, reflecting an old story about how witches traditionally meet up with the Devil at Easter. Other popular festivals are St. Lucia, Walpurgis, and Midsummer's Day. St. Lucia takes place on December 13 and is celebrated across Sweden with "Lucia processions" led by a young girl dressed in white and wearing a special Lucia crown with battery-powered candles. This festival of light brightens up a dark time of year and is a national holiday. Walpurgis, on April 30, dates back to Viking times. It is a celebration of the end of winter and the coming of spring, and is marked by the lighting of huge bonfires across the country. Midsummer is also an old pagan festival, celebrating the longest day of the year. Families and friends meet up to eat herring and potatoes, and, in many places, people dance around a maypole during this celebration.

Focus on: Strindberg

August Strindberg (1849–1912), Sweden's most famous writer and playwright, was born in Stockholm. His realistic and often satirical style of writing about people and situations shocked theater audiences and readers of his stories and novels alike. His novel *The Red Room* (1879) made him famous, as did plays such as *The Father* (1887) and *Miss Julie* (1888). Strindberg was married three times and had difficult and complicated relationships with women throughout his life. In his later years, he experimented with new forms of writing for the stage in works such as *The Dance of Death* (1901).

▲ Boys and girls at a confirmation service in Uppsala Cathedral. The boy is being blessed after receiving a confirmation candle.

CHAPTER 12

Leisure and Tourism

Outdoor sports and recreation are hugely important pastimes in Sweden. The country's sparse population and dramatic and varied scenery make it possible for outdoor activities to be an integral part of the lifestyles of most Swedes. Hiking, ice hockey, running, downhill, and cross-country skiing, sailing, canoeing, cycling, long distance ice-skating, fishing, golf, football, and tennis are all immensely popular.

TRAILS

Sweden is crisscrossed with long-distance trails for cyclists and hikers. One example is the Sverigeleden Bike Trail. This trail runs the length of Sweden, from Helsingborg, in the south, to Karesuando, in the far north, a distance of 1,609 miles (2,590 km). Cycling is very popular on the large islands of Gotland and Öland. Several of Sweden's most popular hiking trails start on the edges of its big cities. For example, the Sörmlandsleden, a 528-mile (850-km) trail, starts on the outskirts of Stockholm. The best known of Sweden's many spectacular mountain trails is the Kungsleden, in northern Norrland. Hikers can take advantage of mountain stations, which offer food and lodging. In the winter, ski trails are marked with red poles for cross-country skiing. Many people flock to downhill ski resorts such as Åre and Sälen.

SPORTING HEROES

The Swedish enthusiasm for active pursuits may explain why so many Swedish athletes

▼ A hiker sits on a rock above the Rapa River Valley in Sarek National Park.

have been successful on the world stage. Swedish tennis legend Björn Borg inspired many of his fellow Swedes to take up tennis, including players such as Stefan Edberg and Mats Wilander. Famous Swedish downhill, or alpine, skiiers include national heroes such as the slalom specialist Ingemar Stenmark and Olympic medalist (in 1992 and 1994) Pernilla Wiberg. Soccer is a popular sport in Sweden, and fans follow their local teams and the national team. The best known Swedish soccer player is Fredrik (Freddie) Ljungberg, who was voted Swedish Midfielder of the Year in 2004, although he currently plays for Arsenal, a British team, rather than a Swedish team.

 Did You Know?

By the time he retired in 1983, tennis player Björn Borg had won 62 men's singles titles.

Focus on: Vasaloppet

Vasaloppet is a famous Swedish cross-country ski race that has its origins in the events of 1520. In that year, Gustav Vasa tried unsuccessfully to persuade the residents of Dalarna, in central Sweden, to rise up against Danish rule. Vasa was forced to flee, closely pursued by Danish troops. The people of Dalarna changed their minds and sent their fastest skiers to catch up with Vasa, which they did at Sälen. Today, the race runs in the opposite direction of Vasa's original journey.

Starting in Sälen, the race ends 56 miles (90 km) away in Mora, which is where Vasa's army eventually defeated the Danes. Since 1922, this cross-country ski race has been held annually on the first Sunday in March (with a few cancellations because of mild winters). In 2005, it attracted more than 15,000 skiers. The fastest anyone has ever skiied the grueling course is a remarkable 3 hours, 38 minutes, and 57 seconds.

◀ Christian Olsson of Sweden on his way to victory in the men's triple jump during the Golden League Athletics Meeting at Rome's Olympic Stadium in July 2004.

TOURISM

The Swedes make the most of their country and its attractions, but they also love to travel abroad. Favorite destinations include Thailand, the United States, Egypt, Australia, and the Canary Islands. Tourism into Sweden has increased dramatically since the 1970s. Many people come for "nature tourism," attracted by Sweden's expanses of unspoiled wilderness. They also come to play golf, go fishing, or take part in more extreme sports, such as mountain biking or sea kayaking. Lapland, in the far north of the country, is a major draw for tourists. In the winter months, people come to view the magnificent aurora borealis, or northern lights, which fills the night sky with dramatic forms in greens, violets, and reds. Lapland also offers the opportunity to learn about Sami life and try out activities such as dogsledding or snowmobiling. At Jukkasjärvi, near Kiruna, tourists can stay in a hotel made entirely of ice. Its walls and even its beds are chipped out of blocks of ice, and guests sleep on thick reindeer skins to keep out the cold.

SWEDEN'S CITIES

In recent years, tourism has expanded in Sweden's cities. Stockholm, Göteborg, and Malmö all have different attractions for visitors. Stockholm is renowned for its beautiful location, and the city is also home to Sweden's Royal Palace and major museums such as the

Tourism in Sweden

- Tourist arrivals, millions: 7.627
- Earnings from tourism in U.S.$: 6,547,999,744
- Tourism as % foreign earnings: 4.9
- Tourist departures, millions: 12.579
- Expenditure on tourism in U.S.$: 9,374,999,552

Source: World Bank

Focus on: Jokkmokk Winter Market

Every year in February, the northern town of Jokkmokk comes alive as it holds its famous winter market. This is a Sami celebration, and it started in 1605 when King Karl IX decreed that marketplaces should be established in northern Sweden. Jokkmokk developed on the site of a Sami winter camp, and its market quickly became an important meeting place for the Sami people. Today, the winter market is still a major Sami festival, with stalls selling Sami handicrafts and performances of Sami music. The week-long market attracts thousands of visitors—80,000 in 2005—from all over the world.

◀ This satellite image shows the aurora borealis over Norway and Sweden.

National Museum of Fine Arts. One of Sweden's most fascinating museums, and a major tourist attraction since it opened in 1990, is the Vasamuseet, or Vasa Museum. The warship *Vasa* capsized in Stockholm Harbor in 1628. More than 300 years later, it was discovered and salvaged. Following years of painstaking conservation and restoration work, it opened to the public. The *Vasa* is the only intact seventeenth-century warship in the world, and the Vasamuseet is the most visited museum in all of Scandinavia.

Göteborg, Sweden's second biggest city, boasts Liseberg, Scandinavia's largest amusement park. The city also offers a wide variety of festivals and events throughout the year. Malmö

has a famous summer festival that attracts more than one million visitors. Malmö is also exploiting the new possibilities opened up by the Öresund Link, which has connected the city more closely with Copenhagen, Denmark.

? Did You Know?

Lapland has one hundred days of midnight sun a year.

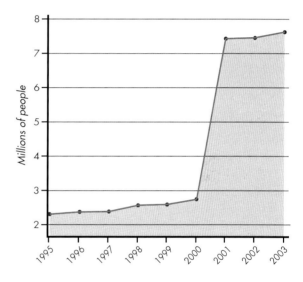

▲ Changes in international tourism, 1995–2003

▶ The Ice Hotel in Jukkasjärvi is made every year from the crystal-clear frozen waters of the Torne River.

CHAPTER 13

Environment and Conservation

The Swedes have a deep-rooted respect for their land. Since ancient times, the country has had a tradition of Allemansrätt, or the Right of Common Access, which allows people to roam the countryside freely and camp anywhere, as long as they do not damage crops or invade other people's privacy. People may also pick wild berries and mushrooms.

NATIONAL PARKS

Sweden was the first country in Europe to set up national parks to protect its country's natural environments. The country's first 9 national parks were founded in 1909, and today there are 28. Together with nature reserves and other special areas, about 8 percent of Sweden's land area is protected. In some parks, camping and lighting fires are not allowed, but people still have the right to roam freely and collect wild produce in these places. About 90 percent of Sweden's national parks is mountainous. The national parks also include environments such as swamps, forests, and archipelago landscapes like those in Ängsö National Park, on the country's east coast. The country's largest parks are Stora Sjöfallet, Sarek, and Padjelanta, in the far north, all of which have dramatic mountain scenery. Sarek has large expanses of true mountain wilderness—without any trails or facilities for visitors.

WILDLIFE

The wilderness areas of northern Sweden provide habitats for a large variety of animals and plants. Animal life in these areas includes wolves, wolverines, lynx, arctic foxes, and bears. There are also many beavers, red deer, elk, and reindeer. One of Sweden's newest national parks, Färnebofjärden, located in central Sweden, is a rich mixture of river, water meadows, and ancient forest that houses more than 100 different species of birds, including woodpeckers

◀ Researchers collect data from a tranquilized bear in Dalarna in 2001.

and owls. Another national park, Abisko, located in the country's far north, is home to the rare Lap orchid. Abisko is the only place in Sweden where this plant grows.

PROTECTING THE ENVIRONMENT

Sweden was one of the first European countries to address the problems of industrial emissions. In 1967, the Swedish government established the Swedish Environmental Protection Agency. Two years later, it passed the Environment Protection Act, which was designed to reduce and control emissions from all types of industry. The act dramatically reduced emissions into the air and water from Sweden's industries, but Sweden continues to suffer from airborne emissions from other countries, over which it has little or no control. In 1999, a new Environmental Code became law. It covers all activities that may harm the environment,

regardless of whether they are carried out by companies or individuals. The code allows tougher punishment than ever before against those who break the law, including fines and imprisonment.

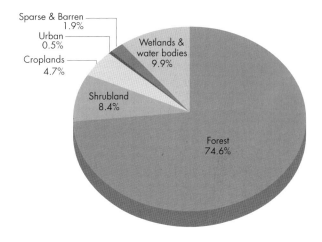

▲ Habitat type as percentage of total area

Sparse & Barren 1.9%
Urban 0.5%
Croplands 4.7%
Wetlands & water bodies 9.9%
Shrubland 8.4%
Forest 74.6%

Focus on: Carl Linnaeus (1707–1778)

Also known as Carl von Linné, Linnaeus was born on a farm in southern Sweden. From a young age, he was fascinated with the plant life around him. Linnaeus studied botany (the science of plants) at Lund and Uppsala universities, and in the 1730s, he traveled to Lapland to study the plant life there. He is celebrated as the scientist who devised the system of classifying plants and animals with two Latin names—for example, *Primula vulgaris*, which means "common primrose." This system of classification is still used today.

▲ A statue of Carl Linnaeus stands in front of the central station in Stockholm.

ENVIRONMENTAL PROBLEMS

While Sweden has cleaned up its industries and tackled the problems of emissions, environmental problems such as acid rain, air and water pollution, and greenhouse gases still remain. Acid rain poisons lakes and other waterways. It is a problem particularly in Sweden's south, although the situation is far better than it was in the 1960s, before controls were introduced.

The majority—80 percent—of greenhouse gases come from energy production and transportation. The number of vehicles in Sweden continues to increase every year, and the vast majority of these vehicles burn the fossil fuels gasoline and diesel. Sweden is encouraging the use of cleaner fuels such as ethanol, natural gas, and biogas, and its sales of vehicles running on these fuels are some of the highest in Europe. Other programs to promote sustainable transportation include joint ownership of pools of cars that can be shared by communities, and tax incentives to encourage people to drive cars that run on cleaner fuels.

In 2006, Stockholm ran a trial for congestion charging, in spite of opposition from residents. This involved making motorists pay a toll to use roads in the center of the city.

THE BALTIC SEA

Water pollution is a particular issue in the Baltic Sea, and Sweden is working very closely with its Baltic region neighbors to address the problem. Discharges from shipping and from countries around the Baltic are causing large areas of the sea to become lifeless in a process called eutrophication. In 1996, Sweden was one of the founding members of Baltic 21, a regional organization that is focusing on the sustainable development of the Baltic Sea.

◀ Swedish Rail is one of the largest users of "green" electricity in Europe. Since 1999, all of its electric trains have been powered by electricity from renewable sources, such as wind power, hydroelectricity, and biofuels.

Environmental and Conservation Data

📂 Forested area as % total land area: 74.6

📂 Protected area as % total land area: 7.2

📂 Number of protected areas: 3,946

SPECIES DIVERSITY

Category	Known species	Threatened species
Mammals	60	7
Breeding birds	259	2
Reptiles	7	n/a
Amphibians	13	n/a
Fish	78	n/a
Plants	1,750	3

Source: World Resources Institute

Focus on: Recycling

Sweden has the highest rate of recycling in Europe. Commercial and domestic waste is sorted and recycled in various ways. People sort their plastic, glass, metal, and waste paper. They also take bigger items, such as electrical appliances or furniture, to waste recycling centers. By law in Sweden, any company that sells certain types of products—for example, packaging, tires, paper, and electronic goods—is also responsible for the collection of its products and the cost of recycling them at the end of their lives. This legislation has made companies think very carefully about the materials they use in their products and packaging.

▲ Cycling is very popular in Stockholm, and it helps reduce air pollution in the city.

CHAPTER 14

Future Challenges

Sweden seems well equipped to face the challenges of the twenty-first century. The country boasts a culture of equality and a strong respect for freedom of speech and democracy.

A MULTICULTURAL SOCIETY

Since the 1950s, Swedes have adjusted to the fact that their country has become increasingly multicultural. During the 1990s, attacks on ethnic minorities by racist groups outraged the vast majority of Swedes, who are passionately opposed to any form of racism. The Swedish government has worked hard to tackle these problems. In 2001, it presented a national action plan to combat racism and discrimination in all areas, and an active integration policy to give "equal rights, responsibilities, and opportunities for all, irrespective of ethnic and cultural background." Nevertheless, disparities between different groups in the population remain. To reduce these differences, the government is embarking on projects to improve education and employment prospects for people from Sweden's immigrant communities. For example, it is providing better training in Swedish for immigrants and also increasing recognition of professional qualifications that have been gained in other counties.

THE EUROPEAN UNION

Since becoming a member of the EU in 1995, Sweden has worked hard to promote the issues it considers important. These include enlargement, greater openness in government, reducing unemployment, and tackling environmental problems. Most Swedes value their country's membership in the EU and regard it as a way of working more closely with their European neighbors over issues such as reducing emissions that cause acid rain and dealing with the problems of pollution in the Baltic Sea. The environment is a high priority for most Swedes, and the country has clear goals and strategies for tackling future environmental problems.

◀ Swedish Muslims pray at a mosque in central Stockholm.

THE ECONOMY

Since its crisis in the early 1990s, Sweden's economy has recovered remarkably well, and its prospects are good for the future. While Sweden's economy relies heavily on exports, the types of products it exports has shifted from products such as steel and timber to the products of its IT and telecommunications industries. Sweden's reliance on exports makes it vulnerable to changes in the worldwide economy and challenges from emerging economic powers such as China and India. Nevertheless, Sweden's vigorous tradition of research and development places many of its companies on the cutting edge in areas such as IT. The future seems bright for Sweden's economy and for the country's people.

Focus on: The Environment

Sweden's government has produced a bill that lists fifteen general targets relating to the environment that it plans to achieve between 2020 and 2025:

1. Reduced climate impact
2. Clean air
3. Natural acidification only (zero acid rain)
4. A non-toxic environment
5. A protective ozone layer
6. A safe radiation environment
7. Zero eutrophication (water pollution)
8. Flourishing lakes and streams
9. Good-quality groundwater
10. A balanced marine environment, flourishing coastal areas and archipelagos
11. Thriving wetlands
12. Sustainable forests
13. A varied agricultural landscape
14. A magnificent mountain landscape
15. A well-built environment (for example, in cities)

▶ This futuristic sculpture, which was designed in 1974 by Edvin Öhrström and is known as the Glass Obelisk, is an example of the mixing of traditional materials and modern design for which Sweden is famous. The 121-ft (37-meter) glass pillar stands in Sergels Torg, a large public square in the center of Stockholm.

Time Line

c.15,000 B.C. Ice covers Sweden.

c.12,000 B.C. The earliest known human habitation in Sweden.

c.1800 B.C. Weapons and other objects made of bronze become widespread.

c. 1500 B.C. Trade routes established as far south as the Danube River.

c.500 B.C. Iron working begins.

A.D. 800 Vikings from southern Scandinavia start to raid and conquer lands overseas.

829 Ansgar, a missionary, brings Christianity to Sweden.

1008 Olof Skötkonung becomes the first Swedish king to be baptized.

1200s Trading towns such as Visby become important centers for the Hanseatic League.

1350 The bubonic plague devastates Sweden's population.

1397 The Kalmar Union unites Sweden, Norway, and Denmark.

1415 Sweden completes conquest of Finland.

1520 Eighty leading Swedish noblemen are executed in Stockholm in the "Stockholm Bloodbath."

1521 The Kalmar Union comes to an end.

1523 Gustav Vasa becomes king of Sweden.

1544 Vasa makes the monarchy hereditary and adopts Lutheranism as the state religion.

1560s–1650s Sweden builds a Baltic Empire.

1611–1632 The reign of military genius King Gustav II Adolf.

1618–1648 The Thirty Years War.

1654 The abdication of Queen Kristina brings the Vasa dynasty to an end.

1735 Carl Linnaeus publishes *Systema Naturae*, in which he presented his system of classification of plants, animals, and minerals.

1810 Napoleon's marshal, Jean Baptiste Bernadotte, is elected as Sweden's king.

1812 Beginning of Sweden's policy of neutrality.

1814 After a short war, Norway becomes part of Sweden.

1850s–1930 Almost 1.5 million Swedes emigrate.

1867–1868 Famine devastates Sweden.

1901 First Nobel Prizes awarded.

1905 Norway gains independence from Sweden.

1914–1918 Sweden remains neutral during World War I.

1921 Swedish women receive the vote.

1939–1945 Sweden remains neutral during World War II.

1946 Sweden becomes a member of the United Nations.

1950s Immigration into Sweden begins.

1953–1961 Swedish diplomat Dag Hammarskjöld is secretary-general of the United Nations.

1986 Assassination of the Swedish prime minister Olof Palme.

1993 First Sami Parliament meets in Kiruna.

1995 Sweden becomes a member of the European Union.

2000 Öresund Link between Malmö and Copenhagen opens; connection between state and religion is broken as Lutheran Church is no longer the national church of Sweden.

2003 Assassination of Foreign Minister Anna Lindh in Stockholm.

2003 Sweden rejects the Euro.

2004 More than 500 Swedes are killed by the giant tsunami that devastates coastlines around the Indian Ocean.

2006 Controversy over the closing of a Web site that showed pictures of the Prophet Muhammad.

Glossary

acid rain a form of pollution caused by sulphur dioxide and nitrogen dioxide emissions dissolving in rainfall

archaeologist a scientist who studies the remains of ancient peoples

archipelago a group of islands

armaments weapons and other military equipment

asylum seekers people who seek refuge in a country to escape persecution in their home country

aurora borealis a phenomenon in the atmosphere around the North Pole that is caused by the interaction of Earth's magnetic field and charged particles from the Sun

Baptist churches Christian churches that believe in adult baptism by total immersion in water

biofuels fuels that are produced from organic matter

Byzantine Empire the eastern part of the Roman Empire, which continued after the fall of the western Roman Empire until the capture of its capital, Constantinople, in 1453

Cold War the period following World War II, lasting from 1945 to 1991, during which the Soviet Union and the United States competed for global superiority by building up their militaries and supporting allies who often fought each other

consensus general agreement

constitution a set of rules and laws according to which a state or organization is governed

democracy a political system in which representatives are chosen by the people in free elections

dynasty a series of rulers from the same family who succeed one another in power

egalitarian believing in the principle that all people are equal and deserve equal rights and opportunities

emissions waste gases and particles discharged into the atmosphere

entrepreneur a businessperson who is willing to take on financial risks in pursuit of profit

eutrophication the process of pollution by which nutrients are carried off agricultural land into the sea where the nutrients feed algae that grow rapidly, depriving other sea life of oxygen and light

formalize to make formal or official

fossil fuels energy sources, such as oil, coal, and gas, that are formed from fossilized plants and animals and release carbon when burned

geothermal energy energy generated by heat deep below Earth's surface

globalization the process by which trade and business is increasingly conducted on a global scale

greenhouse gases gases, such as carbon dioxide and ozone, that play a major role in global warming

Gross Domestic Product (GDP) the total value of goods and services produced within the borders of a country

Hanseatic League (Hansa) an alliance of trading cities in northern Europe between the thirteenth and the seventeenth centuries

hierarchical arranged in a graded or ranked order

hydroelectric power the production of electricity by harnessing the power of moving water

industrialization the process of developing factories and manufacturing on a large scale

Lutheran Church a Protestant Christian church committed to the principles set out by the sixteenth-century reformer Martin Luther

missionary someone who travels to places in order to convert people to his or her religion

Norse an ancient Scandinavian language and culture

racism abuse toward or hatred of people on the grounds of their race or ethnic origin

recession a slump in economic activity

referendum a national vote on a single issue

Reformation the movement in the sixteenth century that challenged the power of the Roman Catholic Church and led to the formation of Protestant churches

rune an ancient form of writing used in Scandinavia

satirical having to do with the use of ridicule in, for example, a cartoon or piece of writing, to point out absurdities in someone's actions

Scandinavia the northern European countries of Sweden, Norway, and Denmark

subsidized paid for by a government to support a particular concern, usually for the public good

trade union an organization that represents the rights of workers in negotiations with employers

tsunami a giant sea surge caused by an earthquake under the ocean

Further Information

BOOKS TO READ

Anderson, Margaret Jean. *Carl Linnaeus: Father of Classification* (Great Minds of Science). Enslow Publishers, 2001.

Binns, Tristan Boyer. *Alfred Nobel: Inventive Thinker* (Great Life Stories). Franklin Watts, 2004.

Docalavich, Heather. *Sweden* (The European Union: Political, Social, and Economic Cooperation). Mason Crest Publishers, 2005.

Hogan, Edward Patrick, and Joan Marie Hogan. *Sweden* (Modern World Nations). Chelsea House, 2006.

Linnea, Sharon. *Raoul Wallenberg: The Man Who Stopped Death.* Sagebrush, 1999.

Schack-Nielsen, Leif. *Sweden* (Countries of the Word). Facts on File, 2005.

Sheldon, Richard N. *Dag Hammarskjold* (World Leaders Past and Present). Chelsea House, 1987.

Wagner, Michele. *Sweden* (Countries of the World). Gareth Stevens, 2001.

USEFUL WEB SITES

CIA World Factbook: Sweden
www.odci.gov/cia/publications/factbook/geos/sw.html

The Government and the Government Offices of Sweden
www.sweden.gov.se

Nobelprize.org
http://nobelprize.org/index.html

Official Web Site of the Sami Parliament
www.sametinget.se

SWEDEN.SE: The Official Gateway to Sweden
www.sweden.se

The Swedish Environmental Protection Agency
www.internat.naturvardsverket.se

Welcome to the Swedish Royal Court
www.royalcourt.se

Publisher's note to educators and parents: Our editors have carefully reviewed these Web sites to ensure that they are suitable for children. Many Web sites change frequently, however, and we cannot guarantee that a site's future contents will continue to meet our high standards of quality and educational value. Be advised that children should be closely supervised whenever they access the Internet.

Index

Page numbers in **bold** indicate pictures.

About the Author

Nicola Barber is the author of many children's non-fiction books specializing in geography, history, and the arts.

DATE DUE

Demco